This book belongs to:

GYO FUJIKAWA'S

Oh, What a Busy Day

STERLING CHILDREN'S BOOKS
New York

STERLING CHILDREN'S BOOKS
New York

An Imprint of Sterling Publishing Co., Inc.
1166 Avenue of the Americas
New York, NY 10036

ISBN 978-1-4027-6819-4

Distributed in Canada by Sterling Publishing Co., Inc.
c/o Canadian Manda Group, 664 Annette Street
Toronto, Ontario M6S 2C8, Canada
Distributed in the United Kingdom by GMC Distribution Services
Castle Place, 166 High Street, Lewes, East Sussex BN7 1XU, England
Distributed in Australia by NewSouth Books
University of New South Wales, Sydney, NSW 2052, Australia

For information about custom editions, special sales, and premium and corporate purchases,
please contact Sterling Special Sales at 800-805-5489 or specialsales@sterlingpublishing.com.

Manufactured in Malaysia

Lot #:
8 10 9
09/19

sterlingpublishing.com

I'm up! I'm up!
It's going to be a busy day . . .
Must brush my teeth,
wash my face, comb my hair,
and get dressed . . .

Then a great, big breakfast!

Through the teeth,
Past the gums,
Look out, stomach!
Here it comes!

Mother, dear,
I sadly fear,
My appetite
is always here!

THEN WE GO OUT TO PLAY

Run, rush,
    chase, and scramble.
Sing, shout,
    laugh, and giggle!

Hop, skip,
    dance, and dawdle.
Fight, cry,
    make up, and smile.

Flip, flop,
    upsy-daisy!
Stop! Chat!
    Gossip a bit!

Bounce, bounce,
    bounce, little ball,
Up, down,
    don't bounce away!

Let's sing!
    La-di-da-da!
        Let's not!
            Yakety-yak-yak!

One, two,
    buckle my shoe.
Let's play
    Hide-and-Go-Seek!

Bushel of wheat, bushel of barley,
All not hid, holler "Charley!"

Bushel of wheat, bushel of rye,
All not hid, holler "I!"

More things to do in
backyards,
front yards,
playgrounds,
and
country meadows!

Well, what do you know?
It's raining!
We'll have to play indoors!

So here we are!

Indoors!

I know what I'm going to do!

Do you?

GUESS WHAT?

Do you ever pretend that
you are something or
someone you're not?

I'm a tree.

Quack! Quack! I'm a duck.

I'm a queen.

I'm Santa Claus.

I'm a sandwich.

I'm a dinosaur.

I'm a peacock.

I'm a house.

I'm a robot.

I'm a turtle.

BEST FRIENDS

Do you have a best friend?
A one and only really true friend?
I do!
She's Jenny!
And she's my very best friend!

Best friends like best
to be with each other,

to talk and play,

and joke
and laugh
at the same things!

Now and then,
  best friends quarrel,
or even have a nasty
  knock-down fight!

And they
  stop speaking
    to each other.

But then,
  they can't stay mad . . .
so they make up,
  happy to be best friends again.

Sometimes
  Jenny and I
    don't talk at all.
We don't have to.
  She knows what I'm thinking
    and I know
    what she's thinking!
Right now,
  Jenny is thinking,
"Let's go
  and work
in the garden!"

And I
  am thinking
    the very same
      thing!

We dig the earth
  and ply the hoe.
  We plant the seeds
  and watch them grow.

The sun and rain
  will help the seeds
  to bud and sprout
  and thrive like weeds.

Then snap a bean,
  sniff geraniums,
  munch a carrot,
  or snip nasturtiums.

SUSIE'S SECRETS

I know some secret hiding places
I'll not tell another person!
Never,
    never,
        never!

I found out where
    the tiny mouse
hurries away to . . . but
    I'll never tell!

I also discovered
    where Major likes
to hide . . . but
    don't worry,
        I won't tell!

The little brown bird
hopes no one will find
her nest . . . I did, but
I'll never tell!

Pussycat doesn't like
to be disturbed
when she's hiding . . . so
I'll never tell!

I know where to look
when little brother
hides . . . well,
I won't tell . . .
but I won't promise!
Ha, ha, ha!

And then there's my own top-secret place.
Don't ask me where, for I'll not tell.
It's my very own, my secret hideaway!

WHEN I'M GROWN UP!

I think I'll be a
ski jumper!

I'm going to be a
tap-dancer.

A football
star!

A clown.

Guess what
I want to be?

An author?

I'd love to be a
mountain climber.

And what do YOU want

A fireman?

A cowboy?

A teacher?

A veterinarian?

A nurse?

An opera singer?

A doctor?

A fisherman?

A construction worker?

A policewoman?

A pilot?

A ballet dancer?

A farmer?

A cook?

An artist?

A pop singer?

An animal trainer?

I'm going to be ME!

KINDNESS

How many kind thoughts
  can a little child have
  for others?

How many kind deeds
  can a little child do
  for others?

How many can you count?
  I'm sure there are a
  hundred and one ways!

Hold on, Mrs. Pussycat!
I'll save your kitten!

How do you feel this morning?

Poor lost dog! . . . Don't worry, I'll find your home for you!

Come, take my hand!

Oops! Let me help!

And a long time ago, Christina Rossetti wrote,

The dear old woman in the lane
    Is sick and sore with pains and aches,
We'll go to her this afternoon,
    And take her tea and eggs and cakes.

We'll stop to make the kettle boil
    And brew some tea and get the tray,
And poach an egg, and toast a cake,
    And wheel her chair around, if we may.

SUMMERTIME

Rock in a hammock.
Go on a hike.
Dunk in a pool.
Have a picnic.
Sleep in a tent.

Lemon juice
   and sugar,
Lots of water,
   lots of ice.

Stir them all
   together.
Stir and swirl them
   all around.

And presto!
   Like magic!
It's puckery,
   delicious,
   ice-cold
   lemonade!

IT'S VERY SAD

When good friends must say goodbye,

when puppy is sick,

when dolly breaks her head,

when the toy duck gets flushed away,

when you're afraid kitty is lost,

and when it pours rain on your picnic.

And here is a very, very sad story . . .

THE BABES IN THE WOOD

My dear, do you know,
How a long time ago,
    Two little children,
Whose names I don't know,
Were stolen away,
On a fine summer's day,
    And left in a wood,
As I've heard people say?

Among the trees high,
Beneath the blue sky,
    They plucked the bright flowers
And watched the birds fly;
Then on blackberries fell,
And strawberries red,
    And when they were weary,
"We'll go home," they said.

And when it was night,
So sad was their plight,
    The sun it went down,
And the moon gave no light.
They sobbed and they sighed,
And they bitterly cried,
    And the poor little things
They lay down and died.

And when they were dead,
The robins so red
    Brought strawberry leaves
And over them spread;
And all the day long,
The green branches among,
    They'd prettily whistle.
And this was their song:
"Poor babes in the wood!
Sweet babes in the wood!
Oh, the sad fate of
The babes in the wood!"

BRAND NEW BABIES

Hello, brand-new baby!
How do you do!
Welcome! Welcome!

Hurry and grow up,
so you can play ball with us!

Waaaah! Waaaah! Waaaah!

My goodness!
There are three new babies
all at once at our house!

Babies need lots of
love and attention!

Sometimes, big brother
gives a helping hand.

They never
seem to
guzzle
enough milk!

It's fun to
watch baby
get bigger
and bigger!

Sleep, little friend, sleep—
When morning comes,
I'll be here
to make you laugh
at my hippity-hop, hop, and hop.

IT'S OKAY

It's okay if you're naughty
   and mischievous and mean—
sometimes . . . But later,
   don't forget to say "I'm sorry!"

And once in a while, it's okay
to pout and sulk and be cross,
But you'll agree that
you look pretty ugly! Right?

It's all right to mope around,
   looking wretched and woebegone.
   Occasionally, that is.
      It's okay!

If your feelings should get hurt,
   so that you cry big, fat tears,
   go ahead! It's only human!

It's okay if you're bashful,
and tongue-tied, shy, and blushing.
There are lots of people
Just as bashful as you and me.

After a bad dream,
isn't it good to wake up
and know that
everything's okay?

And it's disgraceful, but
it's okay to squabble once
in a while. (Although
hardly ever would be better!)

But what can we do
about terrible temper tantrums?

Happiness is a
    gooey mud puddle!
It's okay!
    Jump up and down!
    Splash! Wallow!
    Squish your toes!
Wow!

SOME SILLY OLD JINGLES

Christopher Columbus,
What do you think of that?
A big, fat lady
sat on my hat!

Hi ya, Joe!
What d'ya know?

Oh, Marguerite,
  go wash your feet!
The Board of Health's
  across the street.

Smarty,
Smarty,
thought
you had
a party!

I scream,
  you scream.
We all scream.
  for ice cream.

Ed, Ed,
has a big head!

I should worry,
I should care,
I should marry
a millionaire!

Monkey, monkey,
  sittin' on a rail.
Pickin' his teeth
  with the end of his tail!

Open your mouth
and shut your eyes;
And I'll give you something
to make you wise.

A peanut sat on a railroad track,
His heart was all a-flutter;
Along came a train—the 9:15—
Toot, toot! Peanut butter!

If you are an honest child,
As I think you be,
You'll neither smile nor giggle
When I tickle your knee.

A big bumblebee
Sat on a wall;
He said he could hum,
And that was all.

Betty Boop,
    Ain't she cute?
All she says is
    "Boop boop-a-doop."

Cry, baby, cry,
Stick your finger in your eye;
If your mother asks you why,
Tell her that you want some pie.

Lift the nozzle to your muzzle,
And let it swizzle down your guzzle.

I don't either!

Rose, Rose,
    has big toes;
She carries them
    wherever she goes.

"Flying man, flying man,
Up in the sky,
O where are you going,
Flying so high?"

"Over the mountains
And over the sea!"
"Flying man, flying man,
Can't you take me?"

We Love Animals

See how many
animals
you can name!

Turn this page
to see a dream
come true for some
animal lovers . . .

WHEN COLD WINDS BLOW

Red leaves rustle,
Red leaves bustle,
Red leaves spin,
October's in!

Little witches,
Little ghosts,
Scaring folks—
themselves the most!

Wintery winds,
Whirling snow.
Icy, shivery,
bleak.
Winter winds,
Go away!

Stay here . . .
so warm,
cozy,
and toasty!

It stopped!
It's gone!
  The chilly blasts!
Hooray!
  Where's my hat?
  Where's my coat?
C'mon, everybody . . .
  Let's go!

It's wintertime! It's snowtime!
So get your sleds,
your skates, and snowshoes,
We'll slide and glide and
mush the whole day long!

A FEW CHARMS AND WISHES

Star light, star bright,
First star I see tonight.
I wish I may, I wish I might,
Have the wish I wish tonight.

Break it short,
    bad luck!
Break it long,
    good luck!

He loves me,
    he loves me not.
He loves me,
    he loves me not.

A four-leaf clover for good luck!

Lady Bird, Lady Bird,
Fly away home.
Your house is on fire.
Your children are gone.

Touch blue,
my wish will
come true!

See a pin, pick it up.
All day long you'll have good luck.
See a pin, let it lay.
You'll have bad luck all that day.

Step on a crack,
You'll break your mother's back.

Blow out the candles
with one great WHOOH!
And positively,
your wish'll come true!

Cross my heart,
and hope to die,
If I should tell
A big, fat lie!

SIMPLE WORDS THAT

MAKE THINGS NICE

I DON'T WANT TO PLAY ANY MORE

All day long
    we played together
    and talked of many things.
We had such a good time!
But now, I'm tired.
I want to go home.
So, so long!
    See you tomorrow!

And then, finally,
there's sunset time,
almost suppertime;
the quiet time of day.

And now,
    It's bedtime.
How nice it'll be
    to stretch
    and rest
    and sleep . . .
It has been such
    a busy,
    busy day!